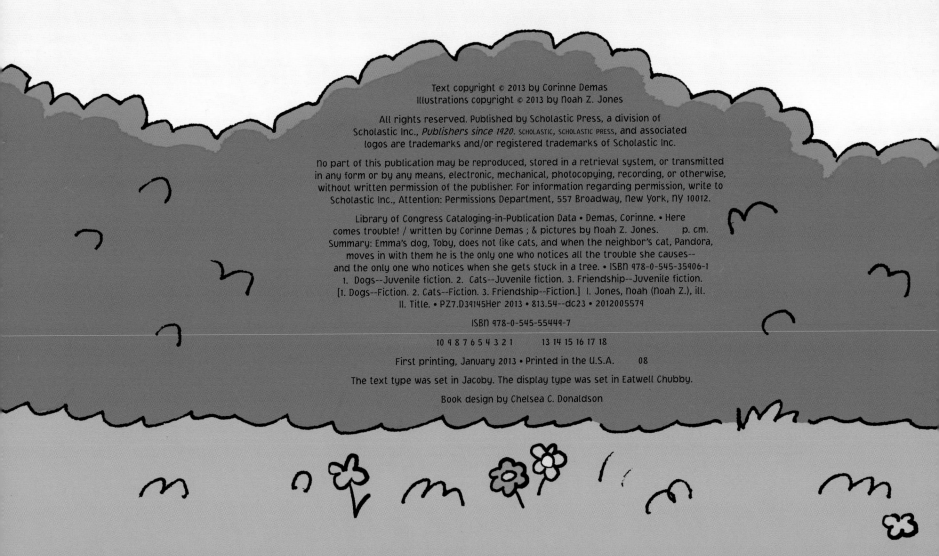

For Morgan and Devon —C.D.
For Sylvie, Eli, and Diane —N.Z.J.

Text copyright © 2013 by Corinne Demas
Illustrations copyright © 2013 by Noah Z. Jones

All rights reserved. Published by Scholastic Press, a division of
Scholastic Inc., *Publishers since 1920.* SCHOLASTIC, SCHOLASTIC PRESS, and associated
logos are trademarks and/or registered trademarks of Scholastic Inc.

Library of Congress Cataloging-in-Publication Data • Demas, Corinne. • Here
comes trouble! / written by Corinne Demas ; & pictures by Noah Z. Jones.   p. cm.
Summary: Emma's dog, Toby, does not like cats, and when the neighbor's cat, Pandora,
moves in with them he is the only one who notices all the trouble she causes--
and the only one who notices when she gets stuck in a tree. • ISBN 978-0-545-35906-1
1. Dogs--Juvenile fiction. 2. Cats--Juvenile fiction. 3. Friendship--Juvenile fiction.
[1. Dogs--Fiction. 2. Cats--Fiction. 3. Friendship--Fiction.] I. Jones, Noah (Noah Z.), ill.
II. Title. • PZ7.D39145Her 2013 • 813.54--dc23 • 2012005579

ISBN 978-0-545-55449-7

10 9 8 7 6 5 4 3 2 1   13 14 15 16 17 18

First printing, January 2013 • Printed in the U.S.A.   08

The text type was set in Jacoby. The display type was set in Eatwell Chubby.

Book design by Chelsea C. Donaldson

HERE COMES TROUBLE!

Written by

Corinne Demas

& Pictures by

Noah Z. Jones

Scholastic Press | New York

Emma's dog, Toby, didn't like cats.

He didn't like slinky cats.

He didn't like spunky cats.

He didn't like snooty cats.
He didn't like snobby cats.

Cats always did exactly what they pleased.
But cats were never in trouble.
Toby was always in trouble.

Pandora, the cat next door,
was slinky
and spunky
and snooty
and snobby.

Worst of all, she didn't pay any attention to Toby.

She didn't pay any attention when he got into the garbage.

She didn't pay any attention when he ran into the road.

And she didn't pay any attention when he dug up the daffodils.

"Our neighbors are going away," said Emma one day.
"And Pandora is coming to stay with us."
Toby stood by the door. He grumbled. He growled.
"Please, Toby," said Emma. "Pandora is our guest. You have to behave."

Pandora slinked by. She didn't look at To
She sat by Emma and licked her paws
Emma scratched her under the chin.
"What a perfect cat you are," said Emm

That afternoon Toby chewed up Pandora's toy mouse.
Pandora didn't notice.

Toby ate all of Pandora's cat food.
Pandora didn't notice.

Toby threw up.
Pandora didn't notice.

The next day Pandora clawed the curtains
and scratched the sofa.
Nobody noticed.

She leaped up on the kitchen counter and sampled the cake.
Nobody noticed.

When Toby leaped up on the kitchen counter,
Emma yelled, "Toby, get down from there right now!"

Pandora pranced by, licking icing off her whiskers.
Something had to be done about that cat!

The next day Pandora pirouetted across the patio
and knocked over five flowerpots.
Nobody noticed.

She chased all the birds from the bird feeder
and scared all the fish in the fish pond.
Nobody noticed.

Pandora climbed a tree.
Nobody noticed.

Pandora couldn't get down.
Nobody noticed.

Except Toby.

Toby barked furiously.
"Be quiet, Toby!" Emma said.

Toby ran in circles around the tree.
"Slow down, Toby!" Emma said.

Toby clawed at the tree trunk.
"Behave yourself, Toby!" Emma said.

Toby waded in the muddy brook
and then ran back toward the house.
Emma ran after him.

Toby ran into the kitchen.
He wrote across the clean kitchen floor
with his muddy paws.

Emma's dad got a ladder. Emma's mom climbed up and got Pandora.

"I hope you won't get into any more trouble,"
said Emma.

Pandora didn't pay
any attention.
She winked at Toby and
slinked off to Emma's room.

Toby trotted right behind her.

Nobody noticed.

Except Pandora.